W9-BVY-509

WHILE I SLEPT

A Richard Jackson Book

While I Slept

story and pictures by
GARY BILEZIKIAN

Orchard Books · New York

Orchard Books, A division of Franklin Watts, Inc.
387 Park Avenue South, New York, NY 10016

Manufactured in the United States of America. Printed by General Offset Company, Inc.
Bound by Horowitz/Rae. Book design by Mina Greenstein
The text of this book is set in 18 pt. Palatino. The illustrations are watercolors.
10 9 8 7 6 5 4 3 2 1

Library of Congress Cataloging-in-Publication Data
Bilezikian, Gary. While I slept.
"A Richard Jackson book."   Summary: A boy sleeps while night noises go on around him.
[1. Night—Fiction. 2. Sleep—Fiction. 3. Sound—Fiction]   I. Title. PZ7.B4925Wh
1990 [E] 90-52514   ISBN 0-531-05875-1 ISBN 0-531-08475-2 (lib. bdg.)

For my grandparents
Rufus and Olive Wheeler

$\mathcal{W}$hile I slept,

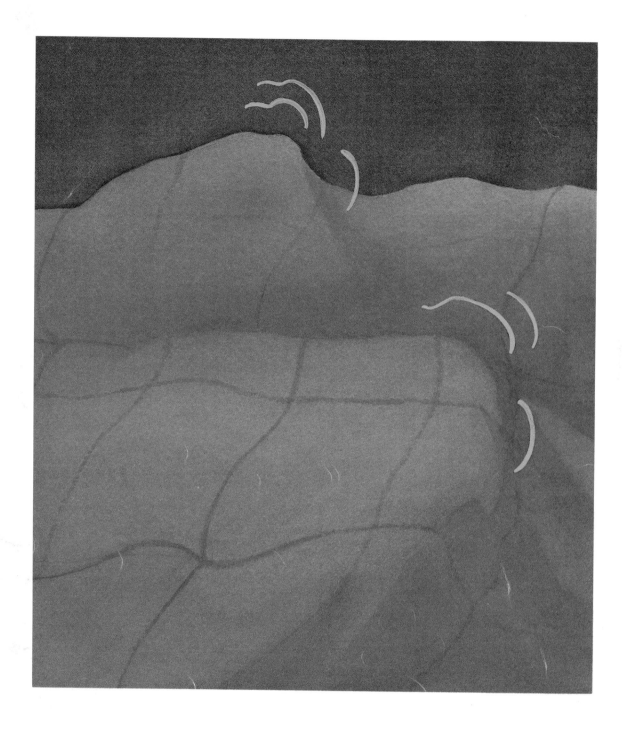

my toes wiggled,

and my bed said:
"creak."

A cat cried:
"me-oww,"

and a dog barked
at the bright moon.

While I slept,
the wind rustled the trees,

a leaf fell,

and the faucet said:

"drip-drip."

The radiator sighed:
"hssss,"

and somewhere the pipes answered:

"clink-clink."

While I slept,

a cricket chirped,

and far off
in the night

a lonely bird sang:

"tweet."

The moon set

while I slept.

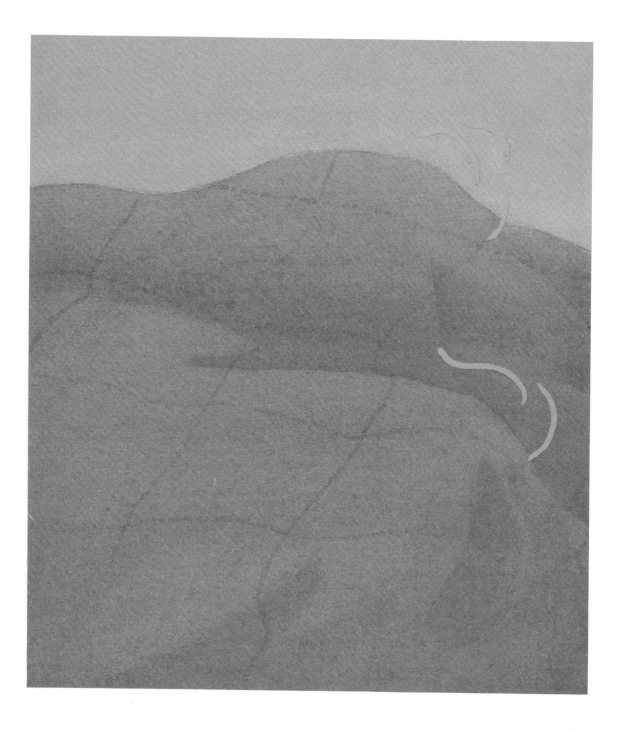

My toes wiggled,

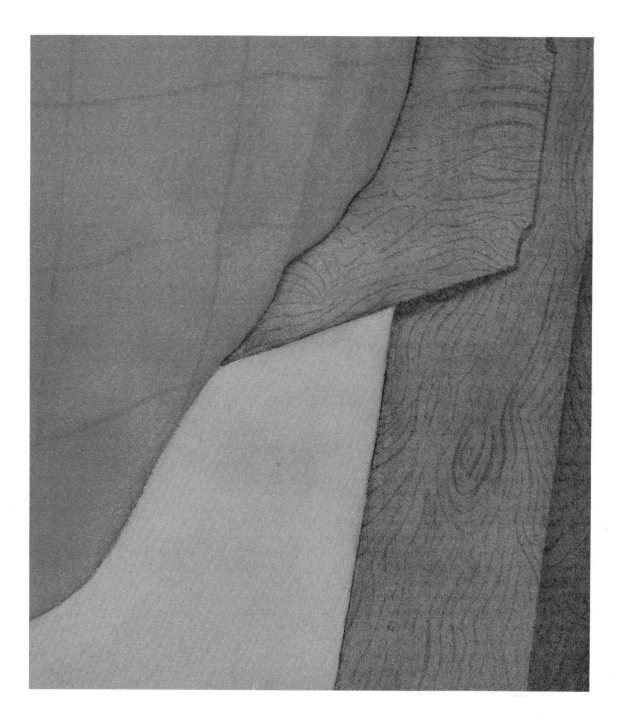

the bed creaked,

and the sun rose in my window to say:

"hello."